D0545355

When 10-year-old Ben Tennyson stumbles upon a mysterious alien device in the woods one summer, little does he realise that his life is set to change - forever.

As soon as the watch-like Omnitrix quite literally gets a grip on him, Ben discovers it gives him the ability to transform into 10 different alien super-beings, each one with awesome powers!

Using the Omnitrix to cause super-powered mischief turns out to be fun, but will Ben learn to use his might to fight for good?

READ ON AND FIND OUT . . .

EGMONT
We bring stories to life

Published in Great Britain 2009
by Egmont UK Limited
239 Kensington High Street, London W8 6SA

Adapted from the animated series by
Glenn Dakin

1 3 5 7 9 10 8 6 4 2

A CIP catalogue record for this title is available from
the British Library

Printed and bound in Great Britain by the CPI Group

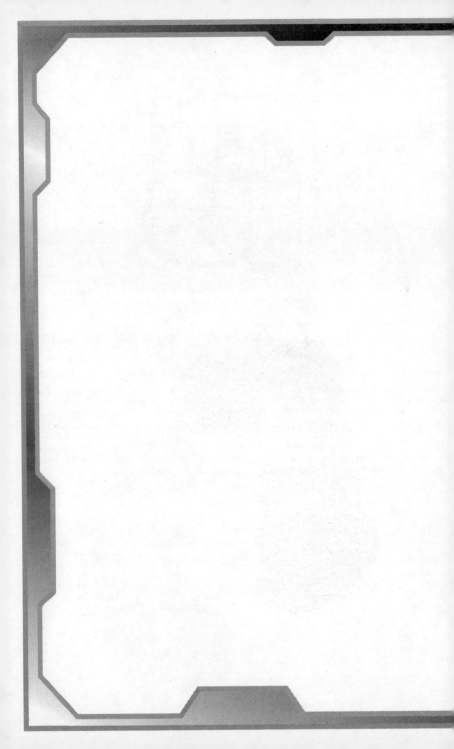

CHAPTER ONE

HANDS UP!

Sleek and menacing, an enormous spaceship moved into orbit round the planet Earth. Its armoured hull bulged with weapons beyond human imagination. A hatch opened and two probes were fired out into space. Inside the

control room, a bug-eyed robot turned to face its master.

'The drones have launched,' said the robot second-in-command, 'equipped with improved tracking systems. They should be able to find the Omnitrix.' A yellow light glowed from a huge metal pod in the centre of the control room, and a creepy voice emerged from within.

'They may find it, but retrieving it will not be easy,' rasped the voice. It sounded half alien, half robot, and all evil. 'Whoever has the Omnitrix continues to be an opponent of extreme danger and inspiring brilliance.'

🟦 🟦 🟦

In a petrol station shop down on Earth, the owner of the Omnitrix was about to show just how brilliant he was. Ben Tennyson, after a long, hungry road trip, had the munchies. He reached out for a box of cookies – from bang in the middle of the display pile.

CRASH! The mountain of cookie boxes fell right down on Ben's cousin Gwen.

'Smooth move, Tennyson,' she groaned, her green eyes flashing. Gwen was used to disasters – both major and minor – whenever her cousin Ben was around. And she knew how to treat them – with typical sarcasm.

The two looked like any other pair of ordinary kids. Gwen was a smart redhead with a cool attitude, in blue sweatshirt and jeans. Ben was a bright-eyed ten-year-old, with a mop of shiny brown hair, and a white T-shirt with a black stripe down the front.

But one thing made these kids different: the chunky black watch on Ben's right wrist was super-cool alien technology, the Omnitrix. It made Ben a hero – and it also made him, and his travelling companions, a target for trouble.

The two cousins stepped out of the shop, back into the hot dry air of New Mexico. The petrol station seemed deserted, apart from one armoured security van parked nearby.

Up ahead, Grandpa Max was washing the dusty windows of The Rust Bucket – the big six-wheeled motorhome they were using for their trip. He was a grey-haired old guy with a fondness for wearing bright tropical shirts. But this grandpa was a lot tougher than he looked – and a lot cooler too.

He smiled as he spotted the little picture Ben had drawn in the dirt on the window – a grumpy face, along with the words: WASH ME.

'Oh, nice artwork, Ben,' he said.

'You know. Makes a statement,' Ben grinned.

BOOM! In a sudden shuddering blast, the back doors of the armoured van parked nearby blew off their hinges. Flames lit the sky and smoke billowed through the air.

'No,' Gwen said, '*that's* a statement!'

Then they appeared – the gang that

had set up this robbery. Ben checked out the threat. There were three crazy-looking bad guys in biker gear, covered in pointy studs. These wackos had painted monster faces on their helmets and sharks' teeth on their energy blasters. Two of the gang jumped into the back of the armoured car, while the other one stood guard.

'What are you looking at?' The gang's leader, a tough cookie called Joey, suddenly noticed that their robbery had a wide-eyed audience.

'Gwen! Ben! Get back!' Grandpa shouted, pushing the kids behind The Rust Bucket for cover. Joey's gun unleashed a blast of pure energy. Grandpa Max dodged out of the way, but was thrown to the floor by the force of the explosion.

'I've *got* to get Grandpa out of there!' Ben exclaimed. He hit the dial of his watch, blinked in the dazzling green glow and braced himself for the change.

The thieves were emptying the van of bank notes when a giant figure loomed above them in the smoke. They were confronted by an alien – a colossal red-skinned monster – who looked as if he worked out a *lot*. Four Arms stared back at them with four bright-orange eyes.

WHOOM! With one mighty blow, Four Arms smashed the petrol station forecourt, creating a shock wave that threw all three bad guys into the air and landed them in a heap.

'Go!' Four Arms bellowed at Grandpa
Max. He hustled to safety with Gwen behind
The Rust Bucket. From out of the security van
staggered a weedy guard in a blue uniform.

'You OK?' asked Four Arms. The guard
took one look at his rescuer and fled, screaming.

'Hmm,' mused Four Arms. 'Wonder if
that's a "yes"?'

Then the gang struck back. Joey blasted a
petrol pump, igniting the gas tank below. A ball
of fire exploded across the forecourt, catching
Four Arms off guard.

'Ben!' cried Grandpa Max.

The three thieves looked into the soaring flames, but saw no sign of their attacker. Suddenly, from out of the column of smoke, leaped Four Arms. Landing with the force of a comet he sent Joey, the gang leader, sprawling across the concrete.

Next, Four Arms picked up the other two thieves and hurled them into the side of the armoured car. While they were still reeling, his big red hands plucked off their helmets.

'Huh?' he stopped in surprise. Two startled girls with blue hair and dark lipstick stared back at him.

'You're all women!' Four Arms continued. 'Look, I don't want to hurt you.' Joey appeared behind Four Arms and zapped him right between the shoulder blades.

'Well, isn't that sweet,' she smirked. Four Arms turned to face her. Joey had taken off her helmet, and was revealed as a purple-haired tomboy, with multiple ear-piercings and sulky fat lips.

'Clobber her!' screamed Gwen from behind The Rust Bucket. At that moment, two robot drones flew out of the smoke overhead. Twin lasers ploughed up the garage forecourt and blew apart what was left of the armoured car.

KA-BLAM! Dollar bills came down in a

great paper shower. Joey grabbed two handfuls
and scrunched them up in despair.

'Hey, this is *my* heist!' she complained.

'You can have it!' snapped back the other
gang members, watching the deadly drones
swoop down to renew their attack. They
were buzzing around Four Arms like angry
mosquitoes.

Joey was too angry at Four Arms to care
about the crazy robot attack. While the big red
hero was distracted, she levelled her blaster at

his back. Grandpa Max grabbed a tyre from a pile nearby and hurled it like a frisbee at Joey's head. **WHUMP!** – it knocked her to the floor.

'Ben, those drones must be after the watch!' Grandpa called out. Joey sprang back up and aimed her blaster at him.

'You'll get yours, old man!' she snarled. The weapon flared to life. Grandpa Max ducked the main blast, but it hit the roof support behind him. Broken concrete tumbled down, sending him crashing to the ground.

'Noooo!' Four Arms roared. This looked serious. The drones attacked again, but they had chosen a bad moment. Playtime was over. Four Arms snatched the flying pests out of the sky and smashed them both together.

'Fly swat!' he growled, hurling the mangled remains at Joey and knocking her off her feet. Four Arms raced to help Grandpa Max up, as Gwen pulled out her mobile phone.

'We need to get him to a hospital,' she

said. 'I'm calling nine one –' Four Arms didn't let her finish. He picked Gwen up in one arm and Grandpa Max in another.

'No time,' he growled. 'Hospital up the street!' With an incredible leap, he bounded away.

❋ ❋ ❋

Left behind in the smoking rubble, Joey climbed to her feet. She picked up a smashed robot drone and peered at it curiously.

'Who were you freaks?' she wondered. Suddenly, the drone sparked to life. It stretched out a probing arm and stuck it into Joey's throat.

'Aargh!' Joey screamed in pain. She was helpless to prevent what happened next. The drone combined with her body, sending out cyber-organic parts into her system. Powerful robot muscles and sharp metal fins sprang up on her arms and legs. Weapon systems connected themselves to a chip in her brain. Red sense globes grew over her face. She was now half robot and half Joey. In fact, she was now Rojo!

Two police cars pulled up, sirens wailing. Four cops leaped out, guns at the ready.

'Freeze!' one of the men shouted. Rojo no longer had to fear the police – her new computer systems told her that. The drone technology summoned two laser blasters. They morphed into position above Rojo's shoulders, and swivelled to target the cop cars.

'I already did my time,' Rojo said. 'It's time you guys paid!' She blasted the two patrol cars into the air. The astonished cops scrambled out of the line of fire.

'This is going to be a blast!' Rojo smirked.

CHAPTER TWO

UNDER CONTROL

The city hospital lay on a sunny corner, nestled among rocky desert hills. Inside, Grandpa Max was in good hands. His bandaged head lay on a comfy pillow, and his plastered leg was winched up to help it mend. Gwen and Ben were not used to seeing him like this. They didn't even know that grandpas could break.

'Your grandfather has suffered a severe blow,' the doctor said. 'He'll be out for several more hours. He also has a broken leg.'

Ben looked glum. In the past, they'd always escaped in the nick of time, by amazing heroics or just dumb luck. But this time Grandpa's luck had run out.

'He's going to be OK, right?' Ben asked. The doctor, a kindly man with a neat black moustache and bright blue shirt was quick to calm Ben's fears.

'For a man his age, he's remarkably strong. He'll be fine after some rest.' The doctor glanced down at the patient's notes. 'Now, it says here he was hit by a car bumper. Did someone back into him?'

Ben thought for a moment.

'Actually, the bumper flew through the air after this robot drone blew up the car.' The doctor looked doubtful.

'A vivid imagination can be a good way to cope with a situation like this,' he said, patting Ben on the shoulder as he walked away. Ben looked back at his grandfather, lying unconscious in bed. For once, he couldn't laugh this adventure off. He had some thinking to do.

※ ※ ※

Up in space, Vilgax was receiving the latest report from his robotic second-in-command. As usual, where the Omnitrix was concerned, the news wasn't good.

'The drones were destroyed,' the robot said. Vilgax seethed inside his recovery pod – the special chamber that repaired and maintained his alien body.

'Send out more!' he barked.

'We may not need to,' the robot replied. 'It seems the drones have somehow merged. I'm receiving one combined signal. And that signal is on the move.'

'Hmmm,' Vilgax paused to consider this surprising report. This was interesting. 'Perhaps one head is better than two.'

In the centre of town, screaming shoppers fled from the jewellery store. Rojo was out to pick up some bling, and she wasn't planning on using her credit card. She surveyed the store, her red sense-globes glowing. Her laser beam cut a perfect circle through a glass display case full of diamond rings. Rojo gleefully grabbed the booty – then cried out as she heard a horrible **SCRUNCH**. Her metal claws had crushed the precious jewels to dust!

'Noooo! They're worthless now!' she cried. She turned in rage, and stomped towards a terrified shop assistant. Suddenly, Rojo was rocked by a sharp pain in the head. She staggered, dazed and bewildered. What was happening to her?

'Listen to me, whoever you are,' a chilling voice spoke inside her mind.

'Where are you?' Rojo gasped. 'Who are you? And how did you get in my head?'

'No questions!' commanded the voice. 'You are here to serve me!'

Rojo tried to move away, but the pain

struck again. She fell to her knees. Suddenly, it seemed to her as if she were falling helplessly through a dark void. She saw a hideous squid-like face before her – except this squid was the size of a house and had glowing red eyes.

'You now possess power you could never have imagined,' the monster said. 'But, unless you find a way to use it, it will be worthless. Fulfil my demand and I will teach you. Fail me, and I will turn you to dust.'

'So what do you want?' asked Rojo. She could see she didn't exactly have a choice here.

'Only one thing,' the alien creature replied. 'A piece of valuable technology missing from my possession. And luckily you are already programmed to find it.'

✵ ✵ ✵

The hospital ward was quiet. Grandpa lay in bed with his bandaged leg raised up, sleeping

quietly. Ben and Gwen sat together by his
bedside.

'Ben, you heard the doctor,' Gwen said.
'He's going to be fine. He's *Grandpa*.'

'I'm worried about him,' Ben sighed.
Gwen's green eyes twinkled with mischief.

'I'd worry more about how some girl
kicked Four Arms's butt,' she teased.

'Hey, heroes don't hit girls!' Ben
protested.

'Good to know,' smiled Gwen, and
smacked Ben in the arm with her fist. In a flash,
Ben smacked her back.

'Ow!' cried Gwen. 'I thought you said –'

Ben interrupted her. 'I'm not in "hero"
mode,' he explained. Then he fell silent again.
He walked into the outside corridor and stared
sadly out of the window.

'You OK?' Gwen asked. 'Normally,
slugging me in the arm would make you feel
much better!' Ben ignored her. He had started

to study the dial of his Omnitrix watch.

'You know, what if I went Upgrade?' he wondered, remembering that that particular alien form that could enter machines and morph them into new, improved ones. 'I could get inside those machines he's hooked up to and see if I could make him better.'

'Ben, that won't work.'

'OK then,' Ben persisted. 'What if I went Ghostfreak? I could meld with him or something. I don't know. I just want to help him, you know?' Again, Ben clicked his watch thoughtfully. This time the central dial popped up, and green energy flashed.

It was enough. The power of the Omnitrix instantly registered in Rojo's brain. She'd been flying over the city, sensors primed for a moment like this. Her drone circuits lit up, sending messages through her upgraded body.

Now Rojo had just one purpose.

She swooped down on the hospital,

her sense-globes zeroing in on the shape of a schoolboy glimpsed through an upper-ward window. Her face lit up with a nasty smile.

'*There* you are!'

CHAPTER THREE

UNFRIENDLY FIRE

'Just relax,' Gwen said, trying to cheer Ben up. They were hanging out in the hospital corridor, just outside Grandpa's room. It was obvious Ben was still pretty upset. 'Everything's going to be OK,' she added brightly. Suddenly, she stood up, her eyes wide with shock.

SMASH! The next moment, Rojo crashed through the window, sending shards of glass flying everywhere. She landed like a big, dark bird of prey.

'Give me the Omnitrix!' she ordered. Ben and Gwen made a run for it.

'You want it? Come and get it!' Ben

taunted. They rounded the corner, dodging and weaving through nurses and porters. Rojo fired her lasers after them, not caring who she hit. One blast tore into a hospital trolley, destroying it in a burst of flames. Hospital staff scrambled for their lives.

'The stairs!' shouted Ben, spotting a nearby stairwell. They raced for the bottom as fast as they could, hoping their foe wouldn't guess where they had gone.

'Ben,' Gwen said, suddenly putting two and two together, 'that *thing* is the girl from the armoured car robbery! It's like she merged with those –'

'Robot drones!' completed Ben.

Suddenly, Rojo appeared at the top of the stairwell. She didn't use the steps. With one incredible, machine-powered leap, she jumped straight to the ground floor, landing where Ben and Gwen had passed only seconds before.

Laser blasts blew chunks out of a door

frame as they dashed out of the hospital into an ambulance park.

'OK, radical thought, but now might be a good time to go hero!' Gwen suggested.

To gain time, Ben ducked behind a row of old ambulances. Gwen followed. A moment later, Rojo was on the scene. She surveyed the row of vehicles. It was pretty clear her enemy was hiding, but she didn't plan on wasting time searching behind every ambulance.

'We can do this the easy way, or the hard way,' she said. Her laser beams targeted the rocky canyon walls above the hospital. Everything was about to change for the ancient boulders that had been lying up there sunning themselves peacefully for centuries. The laser ripped into the rock face and a great landslide headed towards the hospital.

From behind an ambulance, Ben spotted the danger unfolding. He clicked the watch's dial, selecting the powerful shape of Four Arms.

BLEEP! There was a burst of light and there stood Heatblast. The alien hero towered above Gwen, his white-hot body glowing inside a very cool red costume.

'Great. I need muscle and I get an alien candle instead,' groaned Heatblast. The rockslide was getting nearer. There were enough boulders there to pound the hospital into dust.

'If scissors cut paper, fire melts rock, right?' Heatblast raised his glowing hands and unleashed a burst of red-hot flame at the approaching boulders. **WHOOSH!** The rocks caught fire. Now *flaming* boulders were bouncing towards the hospital.

'OK,' admitted Heatblast. 'Definitely not what I had in mind.' He turned to Gwen. 'Go!' he yelled. Now was the time for drastic action. Heatblast zapped each ambulance in turn, and they all sagged together to form a wall of gooey metal. When the boulders came hurtling down, the wall held them back.

'Hospital's safe,' said Heatblast.

'But there are people at the bottom of that canyon!' Gwen cried out. Runaway rocks were still rumbling towards the city below.

'Oh, man, I hate it when you're right!' Heatblast moaned. He sped off after the boulders, but he didn't get far. Rojo streaked down from out of the sky to attack him from behind. She kicked Heatblast sprawling into the dust. Then Rojo powered up her lasers for a close-range attack. But Heatblast beat her to the punch: without a thought, he released a burst of solar fire, blasting her away.

He couldn't worry about his enemy now – he had boulders to catch. Heatblast leaped down the almost vertical wall of the canyon, surfing down the steep slope on a wave of fire. Far below, workmen fixing the road gazed up at the wall of rock hurtling towards them. It only had to cross the river bridge and it would be right on them. They ran, screaming, but there seemed little hope of escape.

SHROOOM! Heatblast unleashed white-hot flames that melted a hole in the great concrete bridge. A smoking chasm opened to welcome the tumbling boulders. One by one, they plunged harmlessly down into the water.

As Heatblast was admiring his work, Rojo flew down and grabbed him in her metal talons. Before he could fight back, she hurled him straight into the back of a dumper truck on a building site below. This time Rojo didn't plan on giving her enemy a chance.

POW, POW, POW! She unleashed one deadly ray blast after another, destroying the truck, the ground it stood on and everything else nearby. Even then she kept on firing into the smoke and flames that had engulfed the site below over and over again.

Finally, she stopped and smiled at the scene of utter devastation she'd caused. Then

the smirk disappeared off her half-robot face
as she heard a rumbling underground. Rock
flew into the air as Heatblast emerged from a
smoking crater. He'd tunnelled away from her
onslaught and was back – raring to fight.

'You want me?' he cried out. 'I'm right
here!'

Recklessly, an enraged Rojo flew at
him. Heatblast ducked out of the way and his
opponent almost crashed into a wrecked fuel
tanker lying in the road. Heatblast finally had

Rojo where he wanted her.

The fiery hero casually tossed a tiny little spark to the floor. It landed in a trail of fuel oil that had spilled from a crack in the tanker.

'See ya!' said Heatblast. A river of fire snaked from where he was standing, straight to the oil tanker behind his foe.

KA-BOOM! Rojo took the full force of the explosion. Meanwhile, Heatblast took off. That crazy robot lady wouldn't be bothering anybody for a while.

Moments later, Ben was back in the hospital checking up on Grandpa. He was awake again, still bandaged and sticking-plastered, but sitting up and keen to get his teeth into Ben's latest problem.

'When I was playing with my watch,' Ben said, 'I must've led her right to you.' He felt bad about being attacked right outside Grandpa's room. Not exactly the peace and quiet needed to recover.

'Since they've moved me to a new room and you haven't gone alien since then, we're safe,' Grandpa Max reasoned.

'Yeah, for now. But what about tomorrow?' Ben said, looking anxious. 'It's getting way too dangerous for you guys to be around me. If I didn't have this watch, none of this weird stuff would be happening.'

'Yeah, but since it won't come off, there's nothing we can do about it,' pointed out Gwen. Ben was gazing off into the distance, still unhappy.

'Maybe – maybe not,' he said, mysteriously. Ben was planning something he daren't tell either of them about.

CHAPTER FOUR

DISAPPEARING ACT

Screaming crowds fled the scene as Rojo stomped through the centre of town. She'd recovered from the impact of the exploding fuel tanker and was back on the warpath, her red eyes scanning the horizon for any sign of her target. Then, suddenly, she was jolted by a surge of power in her mind. Vilgax was making contact again. In the blink of an eye, Rojo felt as though she were floating in a weird unknown realm, face to face with the sinister alien.

'The Omnitrix!' Vilgax shouted. 'Where is it?' But Rojo was more angry than scared this time round.

'I couldn't get it,' she snapped back. 'And

how nice you didn't tell me I'd be fighting a superhero! I'm through!'

She knew she wasn't really though. This game would only be over when Vilgax was through with her. A shock of pain shot through her half-robot body. Then she felt herself tumbling through endless darkness.

'You'll get me the Omnitrix,' Vilgax growled. 'And, if you fail again, your meaningless criminal life will be over. Now, this time, make him come to you.'

✖ ✖ ✖

The hospital ward was silent, except for the soft breathing of Grandpa Max, still lying in his bed, and Gwen, who had fallen asleep in the chair by his side. Quietly, Ben placed a note on the bedside table. He took a final look at the two special people who had stood by him through all his troubles.

'I'm doing this for you, Grandpa,' Ben whispered, although he knew his grandfather couldn't hear him. Then he walked softly out of the room, alone.

Ben sat on the park bench, far away from the hospital. It was a sunny, peaceful afternoon. Over on the grass he saw a couple of people having fun – a boy throwing a football around with his grey-haired grandfather.

'I'm glad we can spend summer together, Grandpa,' the kid said. Ben looked sad. That was how life should be – how his life would never be. Nearby, a lady was sitting in the sun listening to her radio. Then the local news report came on and Ben's ears pricked up.

'Reports say the armoured attacker had incredible fire power and has blown up several police road blocks before arriving at the Police Academy Training Centre just outside of the city . . .'

Ben instantly knew what he had to do.

The blue shadows of late afternoon had crept across the hospital ward. Gwen suddenly woke up with a start and realised that Ben had gone. She spotted his note and read it straight away.

'Dear Grandpa and Gwen,' she read aloud. 'I care about you both too much to keep putting you in danger. It's better this way. Love, Ben.'

Grandpa Max woke up and saw Gwen sitting there with a sad look on her face.

'Gwen, what is it?' he asked. They glanced up to the TV above, to the news report that was in progress. Gwen turned up the volume with the remote.

'The attack at the police training centre continues,' a voice announced. Pictures flashed across the screen of fire, smoke and the ruthless figure of Rojo, blazing a trail of destruction. 'Early reports say several officers have been injured.'

Gwen was in no doubt about where her cousin had sneaked off.

'Ben's gone,' she replied. 'But I think I know where he went. I've got to go, Grandpa.'

'I'm coming too,' said Grandpa Max. He strained all his muscles, but his body would not respond.

'You can't go anywhere,' Gwen told him. He tried to struggle up again without success.

'You can't go alone. It's too dangerous,' Grandpa Max protested. Gwen picked up a small remote control unit and aimed it at the bed. With a swift click she raised the end of the bed a little higher.

'I can't get up now,' Grandpa Max groaned.

'That's the point!' said Gwen. She placed the remote unit on a shelf out of his reach and made her exit – deaf to all her grandfather's attempts to call her back.

✖ ✖ ✖

Outside in the car park, two medics were hopping into the front seats of an ambulance.

'They need us down at the police academy,' one said. They were in such a hurry to get going that they didn't notice Gwen slipping into the back of the vehicle just before it pulled away.

They had no problem locating the trouble spot – the thick smoke was visible from right across town. Rojo stood in the street below, coolly admiring her own demolition job. She swept her lasers across the building again, ripping its stonework apart.

Suddenly, Rojo was smashed off her feet. She looked up and saw a sleek alien form speeding away. It had a pointy black helmet, a stripy tail and whizzed around on weird, ball-like feet. XLR8 was in action!

'Looks like you got this party started without me!' XLR8 said, his bright-green eyes seeming to laugh at her from his neon-blue face.

XLR8 zoomed towards Rojo again, but this time she was ready for him. Stepping to one side, she grabbed him with a robotic claw and swung him on to the ground, then booted him straight into the back of a parked car.

'He wants his Omnitrix – he can have it!' grinned Rojo. 'This is getting fun.'

'Who's "he"?' asked XLR8, sounding a little dazed. Rojo loomed over him, lining up her

lasers to deal out the finishing blow. But XLR8 sprang up and launched a super-speed multiple body-kick at her, rocking her robotic form backwards with his fast-flying feet.

'One good kick deserves another!' he said as a final boot sent Rojo flying. XLR8 activated his visor, which slid down over his face. Now he was ready for anything his opponent could dish out.

A dull rumble made them both turn in surprise. They'd been too busy fighting to notice that the cops at the academy had decided it was time to defend themselves. The vast bulk of a heavily armoured tank lumbered into view, aiming its massive gun turret straight at them.

XLR8 knew what to do in situations like this –
get the heck out of there. **KA-BOOM!** Rojo
took the full blast of the cannon. XLR8 wheeled
around to take stock of the situation.

Thick grey smoke billowed everywhere.
Then out of the dark clouds rolled the tank,
taking aim at XLR8. To his astonishment, the
huge war-machine suddenly rose into the sky.
Rojo was lifting it above her head! She was still
in one piece, still sure of victory, still out to get
the Omnitrix.

'Nice try!' she said, 'but "Speedy" is all
mine!' The tank crew leaped to safety just in
time, as Rojo hurled the massive vehicle at her

foe. It exploded into the tarmac in a mass of mangled metal – but its target had long since disappeared.

XLR8 appeared behind Rojo and hit her with a series of swift punches – punches so fast she had no time to hit back. Once again, Rojo found herself on the ground. This time she had had enough. She knew her foe was too quick for her to beat in hand-to-hand combat, but she did have her deadly laser cannons. She unleashed a searing blast at XLR8, sending him skidding across the ground. This time, she had succeeded. Her enemy was dazed, maybe even out for the count.

An ambulance pulled up on the scene, the driver too blinded by the smoke and dust to see the danger he was heading into.

'Who needs help?' the medic called out. XLR8 sure did. Rojo had lifted him up, and was about to dash his body to the floor. At that moment, Gwen peeped out of the ambulance door, trying to spot her cousin.

XLR8 stirred to life and spotted Gwen –
right in the middle of the combat zone. Like a
streak of light, he zipped out of Rojo's grip and
whisked Gwen away from the scene. Moments
later, they were in a nearby alley.

'What are you doing here?' XLR8 asked,
amazed.

'It's better this way,' Gwen said, with
feeling. 'Sound familiar?' Ben realised she was
quoting his goodbye note. Then the cousins
heard a high-pitched sound they recognised
only too well.

'So does that bleeping,' said XLR8. In a
flash of red energy, he morphed back into a
ten-year-old boy.

'Uh. Just great,' Ben said sarcastically.
Rojo could now be heard, blasting her way
towards them. 'Come on!' Ben said.

Ducking and weaving to avoid the volley
of explosions from behind them, the Tennysons

raced into the academy's shooting range and hid behind a human-shaped target.

'Ben, you can't run away from us,' Gwen said.

'Don't tell me what I can or can't do!' Ben whispered back. 'This is *my* fight – *my* weird watch not yours.' As they spoke, an angry Rojo was scanning the area, shooting up the target range as it had never been blasted before.

'Yeah,' replied Gwen, about as sincere as Ben had ever heard her, 'but you're *my* weird cousin.'

BLAM, BLAM, BLAM! Rojo was taking apart the target range, piece by piece. Soon there would be nowhere left to hide.

'In here!' Gwen hissed. The two cousins raced through a side door into the gymnasium. They looked around for a new hiding place among all the workout machines, balls and weights. In the middle of all the excitement, Gwen's phone rang. Guessing who was on the line, she took the call – and quickly handed it over to Ben.

'It's for you,' she said. Ben looked puzzled.

'Hello?' He couldn't help wondering who on Earth could be calling him at a time like this. Then he cringed, frowned and glared at Gwen. She had put him through to Grandpa Max.

'Can we talk later?' Ben asked. 'I've got an indestructible robot-thing none of my aliens can take out on my tail!'

Back in the hospital, Grandpa Max was on the road to recovery. He was sitting up in bed, clear-eyed, that old determined look on his face.

He spoke urgently into his mobile phone.

'Ben, if you can't destroy it from the outside, take it down from the inside.'

Ben's eyes lit up. He realised exactly what Grandpa Max was driving at.

'That's it!' he cried out. 'Thanks!' He flipped the phone shut and handed it to Gwen. She had that familiar sparkle in her big green eyes.

'Looks like *you're* not better off without Grandpa, huh?'

Outside, Rojo was closing in. Her prey had somehow escaped her so far, but her drone computers told her there was only one place left for her foe to hide. She flew towards the gym.

Inside, Ben was crouching behind a pillar, clicking the dial on his Omnitrix. As usual, it wasn't playing ball. **THWACK!** Ben started to thump the dial, with increasing urgency. Yesss! He'd finally done it! In a blinding flash, a big, flowing shape rose up in place of the ten-year-old boy. It had a circular face and flashing green circuits dotted about its black-and-white body. Upgrade was ready to go to work!

CRASH! Rojo made a surprise entrance through the roof, enjoying the destruction she was causing. She floated through the silent gym, scanning for her target. She didn't see Gwen cowering behind a weights machine, and she certainly didn't see Upgrade spread out across the ceiling like an enormous high-tech pancake.

FLUMP! Down Ben fell, covering Rojo's head and sinking into her armour, invading her computer systems. Upgrade could enter, explore and improve any device. He could also wreck anything.

'Agghh!' Rojo cried out in pain. For the first time in the whole battle she realised she was in big trouble. Upgrade was breaking down Rojo's defences, preparing to disable her weapons, shut down her computers, make her useless.

   Suddenly, Upgrade clutched at his head,
crying out in pain. He'd entered Rojo's computer
mind – a brain programmed to make contact
with Vilgax. Ben was about to come face to face
with his deadliest enemy.

CHAPTER SIX

SHUT DOWN

Upgrade felt like he was floating through dark space, away from everything he knew, unable to fight back. Before him was an enormous squid-like head, its creepy red eyes burning into him. He was being held by an alien claw, as if he were just a toy.

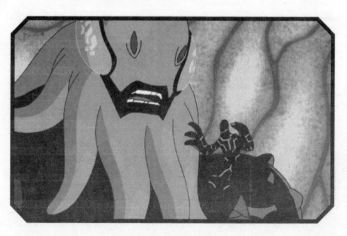

'Listen to every word,' said a cold alien voice. 'Be afraid. You cannot run, you cannot hide from me. I will find you. And, when I do, I will retrieve my Omnitrix and destroy you!'

Suddenly, Vilgax disappeared. The link between their minds was broken. Rojo began to struggle. She jerked her head back and threw Upgrade off her. The big, floppy alien hit a concrete pillar and slid down it.

Upgrade was out of Rojo's system, but by no means out of the fight. He quickly melded with an exercise machine, reached out with his metal handles and grabbed Rojo's head, beating it against his own solid frame.

'Time to work out!' Upgrade said as Rojo fell on to a treadmill machine. Upgrade swiftly melded with that, and sped up the walking belt to catapult Rojo head first into another machine. **WHAM!** She was on the ropes at last.

A groggy Rojo stumbled away just as a team of police marksmen entered the gym. They were all wearing protective masks and carrying the latest high-tech laser rifles.

'Duck!' screamed Gwen, who was the first to spot them. **BLAM, BLAM, BLAM!** – the cops were in no mood to take prisoners. Blast after blast rocked Rojo's armoured body. While she was distracted, Upgrade leaped at her for a final time, covering her like a wad of soft bubblegum.

'Now, this won't hurt a bit,' he said, seeping into each and every one of her circuits.

'Aaggh!' cried Rojo. 'Get out of me!'

Upgrade invaded her systems at lightning speed, did as much damage as he could, and then ejected himself straight out again.

'OK, I lied,' he said, leaving Rojo a shattered, quivering wreck.

The police team stood back, weapons at the ready. But they needn't have bothered – Rojo would never attack anyone again. She cracked, she shook, she wobbled and then she fell to bits.

One by one, her drone implants flew off and crashed to the ground. Her body was restored to its original form. Even the energy blaster she had used in the robbery earlier in the day returned to its original shape and clattered to the ground.

'I-I'm normal,' she moaned, still in a daze. Her clothes were a little ragged, her pride a little dented, but she was back in one piece, and as full of bad attitude as ever.

'Abnormal's way more like it,' commented

Upgrade. Joey had spotted her weapon and was already edging her way towards it.

'Look, I don't know what came over me,' she said in a pathetic, put-on voice. 'Please, you've got to help me. I'm just a girl.' As Upgrade hesitated, Joey snatched up her gun and aimed it at him.

'Guess what?' came a voice behind her. It was Gwen, flying straight at Joey, with her best *tae kwon do* kick. 'So am I!'

Joey crashed back into a pillar, and the whole gym began to shudder and crumble to the floor.

'Gwen, we've got to go!' shouted Upgrade as the place started to come down around their ears. Gwen and the police team fled, but Upgrade bent down and picked up the unconscious Joey and carried her out.

'She's all yours,' Upgrade said, in true hero style, and handed the defeated Joey over to the cops.

Night had fallen. Upgrade and Gwen tasted the cool air and stood side by side under the starlit sky. The end of another adventure always tasted sweet.

A few minutes later, the Tennysons were reunited. The Rust Bucket was standing in the hospital car park, and lumbering towards it was a big, grey-haired guy, in a bright red tropical shirt, on a pair of crutches.

'It's good to get out of here and get back on the road,' said Grandpa Max. But Gwen still had an unanswered question.

'So, Ben, what happened back there in the gym? It's like you were possessed or something.'

'I don't know,' Ben replied. 'It was like when I went Upgrade I saw this alien. We were both floating through space and he was talking to me. It looked kind of like he had this octopus on his head. He said I should be afraid.'

His grandfather frowned. The description of the weird vision had obviously bothered him.

'Grandpa,' Ben said. 'You look worried.'

'I'm fine,' said Grandpa Max, hiding his true feelings. 'You'll be fine too. As long as we stay together.' Ben smiled, remembering the note he had left them just hours before. From now on, walking away from his family was no longer an option.

'Sounds good to me,' he said.

Grandpa Max stared up at the twinkling stars. They looked beautiful. But he knew that somewhere up there, a pair of evil red eyes was looking right back down at the Earth – forever hunting the Omnitrix.

BOOK COLLECTION

HAVE YOU SEEN THEM ALL?

Ben 10 Alien Force Annual 2010	978 1 4052 4653 8; £7.99
Ben 10 Alien Force colour storybook 1 (Ben 10 Returns Part 1/Part 2)	978 1 4052 4799 3; £4.99
Ben 10 Alien Force colour storybook 2 (The Gauntlet/Be-Knighted)	978 1 4052 4800 6; £4.99
Ben 10 Amazing 3D Hero Vision	978 1 4052 4413 8; £3.99
Ben 10 Puzzle and Quiz Book	978 1 4052 4492 3; £3.99
Ben 10 Magnet Book	978 1 4052 4599 9; £5.99
Ben 10 All Action Stories & Flicker Book	978 1 4052 4512 8; £4.99
Ben 10 comic book 1 (And Then There Were 10)	978 1 4052 4663 7; £4.99
Ben 10 comic book 2 (Washington B.C.)	978 1 4052 4664 4; £4.99
Ben 10 comic book 3 (The Krakken)	978 1 4052 4804 4; £4.99

Ben 10 comic book 4
(Permanent Retirement)   978 1 4052 4805 1; £4.99

Ben 10 chapter storybook 1
(And Then There Were 10/Kevin 11)   978 1 4052 4467 1; £3.99

Ben 10 chapter storybook 2
(The Alliance/Secrets)   978 1 4052 4468 8; £3.99

Ben 10 chapter storybook 3
(Truth/Framed)   978 1 4052 4672 9; £4.99

Ben 10 chapter storybook 4
(The Galactic Enforcers/Ultimate Weapon) 978 1 4052 4673 6; £4.99

COMING SOON ...
3 COOL NEW BEN 10 BOOKS!

Ben 10 Alien Force Extreme (Pop-Up) 978 1 4052 4852 5; £14.99

Ben 10 Alien Force chapter storybook 1
(All That Glitters/Max Out)   978 1 4052 5006 1; £4.99

Ben 10 Alien Force chapter storybook 2
(Paradox/Plumbers' Helpers)   978 1 4052 5007 8; £4.99

Visit Egmont.co.uk